CELINE DION
LOVED ME BACK TO LIFE

MW00560736

CONTENTS

Alfred Music
P.O. Box 10003
Van Nuys, CA 91410-0003
alfred.com

Printed in USA.

ISBN-10: 1-4706-1414-6
ISBN-13: 978-1-4706-1414-0

Photography by: Alix Malka
Art Direction by: Maria Paula Marulanda

LOVED ME BACK TO LIFE

Words and Music by
DENARIUS MOTES, HASHAM HUSSAIN
and SIA FURLER

Moderately slow rock ♩ = 76

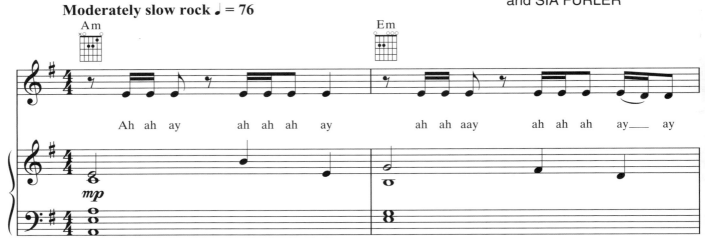

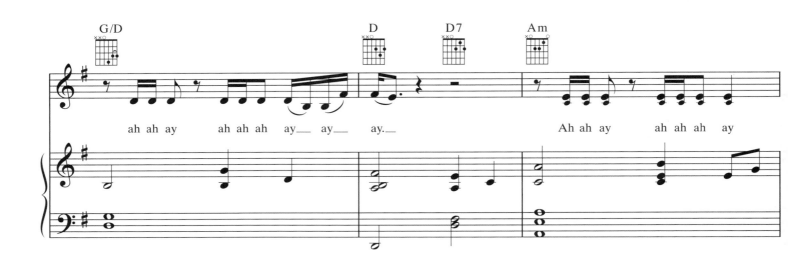

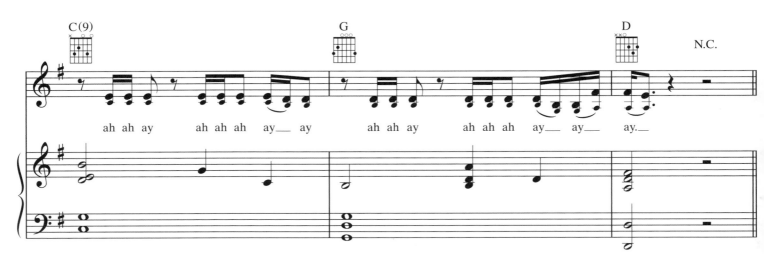

Love Me Back To Life - 9 - 1

Chorus:

SOMEBODY LOVES SOMEBODY

Words and Music by
JOHAN FRANSSON, TOBIAS LUNDGREN,
TIM LARSSON and AUDRA MAE

12

Chorus:

some-bod-y loves some-bod-y, that's the way it's sup-posed_ to_ be. 'Cause you know no-bod-y else would

put up with your games. Oh,_ I don't be-lieve in lov-ing you. Don't wan-na go._ No!_

That's not the way it is when some-bod-y loves some-bod-y._

(Eh_ eh_ eh_ eh_

Chorus:

INCREDIBLE

Words and Music by
ANDREW GOLDSTEIN, SHAFFER SMITH
and EMANUEL KIRIAKOU

22

Incredible - 8 - 5

oh_____ oh_____

oh_____ oh_____

oh_____ oh.

Celine & Ne-Yo:

Let's give them some-thing a - maz - ing!_____

WATER AND A FLAME

Words and Music by
FRANCIS "EG" WHITE
and DANIEL MARRIWEATHER

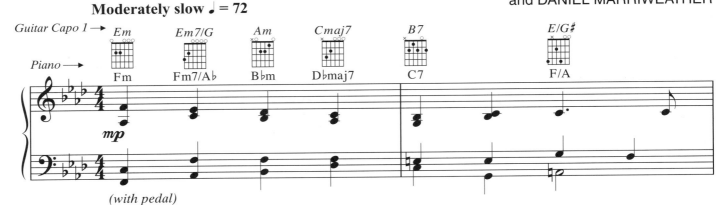

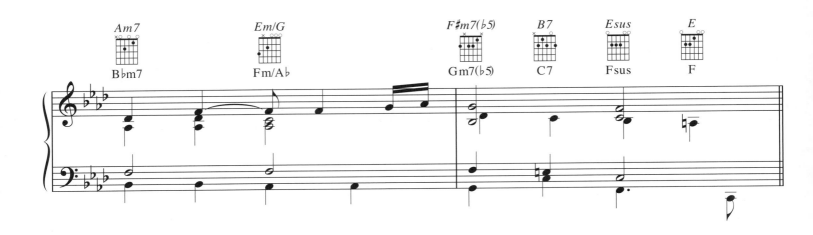

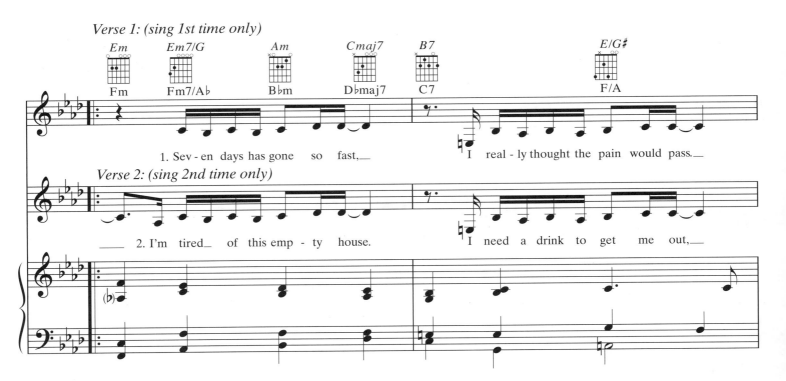

1. Sev-en days has gone so fast,__ I real-ly thought the pain would pass.__

Verse 2: (sing 2nd time only)

2. I'm tired__ of this emp-ty house. I need a drink to get me out,__

30

BREAKAWAY

Words and Music by
JOHAN FRANSSON, TOBIAS LUNDGREN,
TIM LARSSON and AUDRA MAE

Moderate rock ♩ = 116

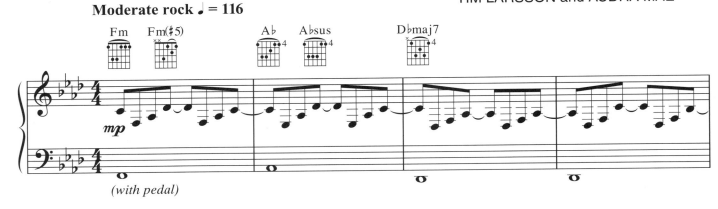

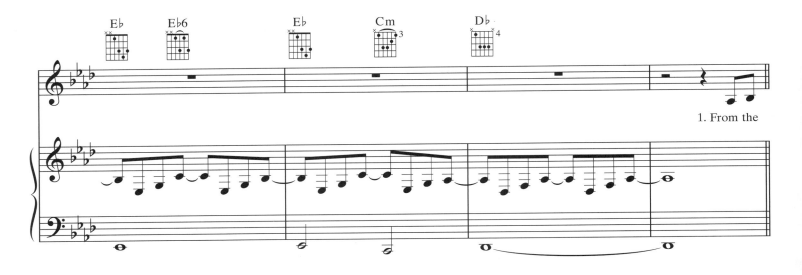

1. From the

Verse:

fire_____ in____ your words_____ to the dag - ger in____ your eye,_____

(2.) true____ what peo - ple say,_____ that it's dark - est be - fore dawn?

34

38

Breakaway - 9 - 7

40

DIDN'T KNOW LOVE

Words and Music by
FRANCIS "EG" WHITE,
JESSI ALEXANDER and TOMMY LEE JAMES

Moderately slow rock ♩ = 76

Didn't Know Love - 7 - 1

44

SAVE YOUR SOUL

Words and Music by
DANIEL MURCIA

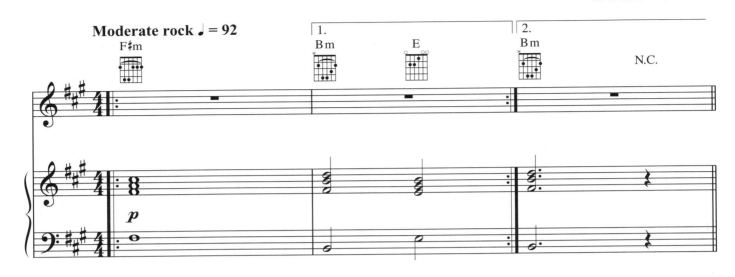

Verse 1:

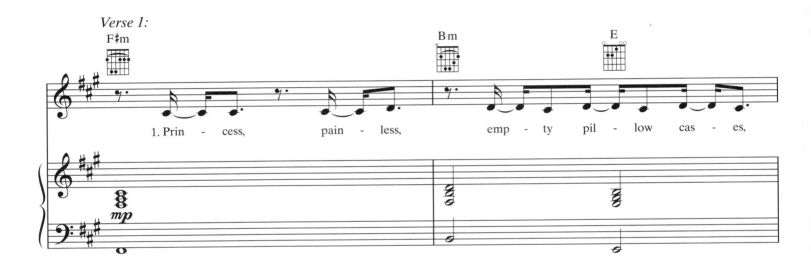

1. Prin - cess, pain - less, emp - ty pil - low cas - es,

one ___ love ___ too ___ blind. ___

Save Your Soul - 8 - 1

Save Your Soul - 8 - 2

51

Save Your Soul - 8 - 4

Chorus:

THANK YOU

Words and Music by
SHAFFER SMITH, JESSE WILSON
and REGINAL SMITH

* *Original recording in D♭, guitars tuned down 1/2 step.*

Thank You - 7 - 1

58

60

OVERJOYED

Words and Music by
STEVIE WONDER

64

Overjoyed - 9 - 2

66

- 9 - 4

70

THANKFUL

Words and Music by
DANA PARISH
and ANDREW HOLLANDER

74

Chorus:

thank-ful____ to be____ here, thank-ful____ to feel____ clear,

thank-ful my prayers have been an-swered._____ I'm

thank-ful____ you lis-tened, thank-ful____ to heav-en,

thank-ful____ for feel-in'____ a-live,_____ a-gain,_

76

Thankful - 8 - 5

Thank-ful___ for feel-in' a - live___ a - gain.___

oh.___

Thank-ful that hearts al - ways mend.___

Thank-ful___ my heart al - ways___ mends.___

Thankful - 8 - 8

AT SEVENTEEN

Words and Music by
JANIS IAN

*Omit cue size notes first time

82

ALWAYS BE YOUR GIRL

Words and Music by
DANA PARISH
and ANDREW HOLLANDER

88

90

HOW DO YOU KEEP THE MUSIC PLAYING

Lyrics by
ALAN and MARILYN BERGMAN

Music by
MICHEL LEGRAND

94

95

How Do You Keep the Music Playing - 6 - 4

How Do You Keep the Music Playing - 6 - 6

UNFINISHED SONGS

Words and Music by
DIANE WARREN

Moderate pop rock ♩ = 95

Unfinished Songs - 5 - 2

100

Unfinished Songs - 5 - 3

LULLABYE
(GOODNIGHT, MY ANGEL)

Words and Music by
BILLY JOEL

Freely

Verse 3:

Some-day we'll all be gone but lull-a-byes go on and on.

Broadly

The nev-er die, that's how you and I will

be.